VICTORY ★ SCHOOL SUPERSTARS

STONE ARCH BOOKS
a capstone imprint

Sports Illustrated KIDS

I Couldn't Land a Bunny Hop

by **Chris Kreie**
illustrated by **Jorge Santillan**

STONE ARCH BOOKS
a capstone imprint

Sports Illustrated KIDS *I Couldn't Land a Bunny Hop*
is published by Stone Arch Books — A Capstone Imprint
1710 Roe Crest Drive,
North Mankato, MN 56003
www.capstonepub.com

Art Director: Bob Lentz
Graphic Designer: Hilary Wacholz
Production Specialist: Michelle Biedscheid

Timeline photo credits: Library of Congress (top right);
Shutterstock/Inc (top left), skvoor (middle right), Suzanne Tucker
(middle left); Sports Illustrated/Robert Beck (bottom).

Printed in the United States of America in
North Mankato, Minnesota.
052017
010554R

Library of Congress Cataloging-in-Publication Data
Kreie, Chris.
   I couldn't land a bunny hop / by Chris Kreie; illustrated by Jorge H. Santillan.
   p. cm. — (Sports illustrated kids. Victory School superstars)
   Summary: When Josh is asked to try out for the school BMX team, he is not
sure that he can do any of the tricks--can practice make perfect in time for the
Metro Games?
   ISBN: 978-1-4342-3762-0 (library binding)
   ISBN: 978-1-4342-3865-8 (paperback)
   ISBN: 978-1-4342-4985-2 (e-book)
   1. Bicycle motocross—Juvenile fiction. 2. Stunt cycling—Juvenile fiction. 3.
Competition (Psychology)—Juvenile fiction. 4. Teamwork (Sports)—Juvenile
fiction. [1. Bicycle motocross--Fiction. 2. Stunt cycling--Fiction. 3. Competition
(Psychology)—Fiction. 4. Teamwork (Sports)—Fiction.] I. Santillan, Jorge,
ill. II. Title. III. Title: I could not land a bunny hop. IV. Series: Sports Illustrated
kids. Victory School superstars.
PZ7.K8793Iah 2012
[Fic]—dc23   2011032818

TABLE of CONTENTS

JOSH CHAMPS

BMX

AGE: 10
GRADE: 4
SUPER SPORTS ABILITY: Super Skating

VICTORY SCHOOL SUPERSTARS

CARMEN

DANNY

ALICIA

KENZIE

TYLER

VICTORY SCHOOL MAP

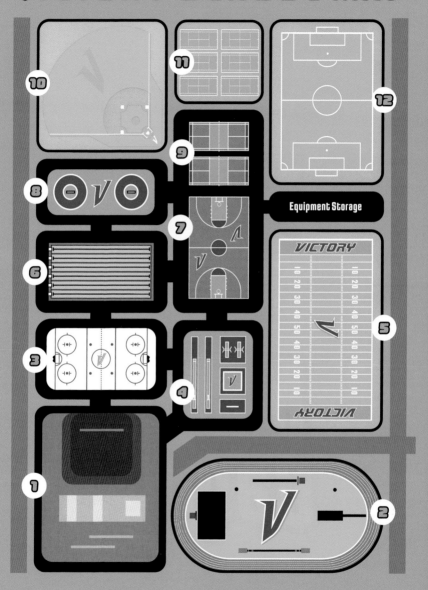

1. BMX/Skateboarding
2. Track and Field
3. Hockey/Figure Skating
4. Gymnastics
5. Football
6. Swimming
7. Basketball
8. Wrestling
9. Volleyball
10. Baseball/Softball
11. Tennis
12. Soccer

Metro
Games

"I don't know about you, but after those three tests today, I'm glad that school is over," I say to my pal Kenzie. We head down the crowded hallway of Victory School for Super Athletes.

Suddenly Kenzie freezes.

"Look at this," she says. She points to a poster on the wall. "Victory School will have a team at the BMX Metro Games this year!"

"Cool," I say.

"It's more than cool," says Kenzie. "It's awesome! Do you want to do it with me? Tryouts are next week."

"I don't know anything about BMX," I say. Hockey is my game, thanks to my super skating ability. Everyone at Victory has a super sports skill that makes us tough to beat.

"Come on, Josh. You're good at every sport you try," says Kenzie. "I'm sure you would be good at BMX, too."

Kenzie has a point. I've tried lots of sports, including soccer and wakeboarding. I wasn't very good at either of them right away. But with a little practice, I got a lot better.

"Sure, why not?" I say. Kenzie and I share a high-five.

"Let's go to the bike park and practice," says Kenzie. She takes off down the hall.

"Now?" I shout.

"No time like the present!" she yells back.

"Let's at least go home and change," I say.

"If you insist," she says, and she leaves me in the dust.

Crash!

At the bike park, Kenzie rips it up. Each trick she does is more amazing than the last. I had no idea she was so good.

A group of boys is also watching her. I recognize Kirk from my science class. They have stopped riding to check out Kenzie's moves.

Kenzie takes off over the largest ramp at the park. She soars through the air and extends her arms out before coming down in a perfect landing.

"You're awesome!" I say.

"Your turn," says Kenzie. She is out of breath.

I'm nervous. The guys are still watching us. I make sure my helmet and pads are on tight. Then I set up in front of a short ramp.

I pedal toward it, but I'm scared. I'm not going fast enough to get any air. My bike cruises gently up one side of the ramp, across the flat part, and down the other side.

Kirk and his friends laugh at me.

I try again, but I'm still scared. I only get an inch or two of air.

The guys laugh even louder.

I want to prove to them that I can do it. I put my head down and pedal as fast as I can. My bike hits the lip of the ramp, and I fly through the air. I panic. My bike goes one way. I go another. I crash hard to the ground.

Kirk and his friends shake their heads and pedal away. Kenzie rushes over to me.

"Are you okay?" she asks.

"I'm fine," I say. "But you should practice without me. I'm holding you back."

"We're in this together," Kenzie says, helping me up. "I know you can learn."

"I'm not so sure," I say and walk slowly over to get my bike. "At this point, I couldn't even land a bunny hop."

Flatland

Kenzie and I are at the Victory ice rink the next day. It's Saturday. We have the whole day to do whatever we want.

I skate toward the center of the ice and go into a fast spin. I hold the move for almost a minute then glide forward on one skate. My left leg is pointed toward the ceiling. The rest of my body is leaning forward. My arms make it look like I'm flying.

"That's it!" Kenzie shouts. I lose my balance and almost fall over.

"What?" I ask.

"Come on. Let's go to my house," says Kenzie skating toward the exit. "I have an idea."

At Kenzie's house, she pulls up a BMX website on her computer. On the screen, a rider moves across an empty tennis court. He twists and spins his bike like it's a dance. I can't turn away.

"This is the most awesome thing I've ever seen!" I say.

"It's called flatland BMX," says Kenzie.

"What about the jumps?" I ask. "And where are the ramps?"

"There aren't any," she says. "Riders never leave the ground."

"Really?" I say. "That's my kind of BMX."

"You would be great at this," Kenzie says.

"Some of the moves even look like skating spins," I say.

"I know, right?" Kenzie gets up from her chair. "Are you ready to try it?"

"Sure, why not?" I say. "I can't possibly do any worse than I did at the park."

"Let's go then," she says.

I'm excited. This time, I leave Kenzie in the dust.

Tryouts

I practice some flatland moves on Kenzie's driveway. When I master one, we go watch another one on her computer.

After a couple hours, I have learned ten tricks. I even start inventing some of my own. I can spin and lean and twirl my bike in all sorts of amazing ways. We work together all day.

"I knew you would be good at this," Kenzie says. "Your balance is unbelievable."

"It reminds me of skating," I say.

We practice every day after school for the rest of the week. Then it's time for the Metro Games tryouts.

Dozens of kids are gathered at the park. Right away we see Kirk and his buddies.

He looks at me and laughs. "You're trying out?" he says. "There is no way you're going to make the team."

I look at Kenzie then smile at Kirk. I'm confident because of everything I have learned this week. "Just watch me," I say. "I think you'll be surprised."

Tryouts begin. Kirk is really good. He and Kenzie make it onto the Victory School team. Two of Kirk's friends, Casey and Will, also make it.

My event is last. The team only needs one flatland rider. I use all the moves I learned this week, and I earn the last spot on the Victory team. I'm totally stoked!

The five of us gather for a photo. "What do you think of me now?" I ask Kirk with a grin.

"You're not as bad as I thought," says Kirk, grinning. "Truce?" He holds out his hand.

I shake it. "Sure thing . . . teammate," I say.

The Big Day

The day of the BMX Metro Games is here. Our team gathers together at the park. We look cool in our red Victory T-shirts and our team helmets.

A large crowd is seated in the bleachers around the park. I swallow hard as I think about performing in front of all these people.

There will be three events. Kirk and Kenzie are competing in the park event. They will bike through the park course, jumping over ramps and doing as many tricks as they can.

Casey and Will are doing the vert event. They will try for big air and tricks in the halfpipe. Of course, I'll be doing the flatland.

I look over at the blacktop where I'll be competing. Riders from other teams are warming up. They do one unbelievable trick after another.

Kenzie catches me watching them. "Don't worry about those guys," she says. "Just do your best. That's all you can do."

"Even my best can't beat those guys," I say.

"Let's go," Kenzie says. "The vert event is starting."

Casey and Will do an awesome job in the halfpipe. Casey gets the biggest air of anyone and receives the top score. Will finishes fifth. It's good enough to put our team in second place.

The park event is next. Of course Kenzie rocks it out. She pedals around the course, gracefully doing trick after trick. She gets more air with each jump.

Kirk also shines. He lands two 360 spins. Kenzie wins first place. Kirk gets third. Our Victory team is now in first place.

I'm happy for my teammates, but I can't celebrate with them yet. I'm too worried about my own ride. Flatland is the last event. I feel even more pressure than before. If I don't perform well, I could cost our team the cup.

My Routine

The rider from the Golden Comets is first in the flatland event. He does at least a dozen perfect moves including an amazing one-handed wheelie.

The next rider is from the Fighting Eagles. She is even better. She does one trick where she hops on the front wheel of her bike like a pogo stick for at least thirty seconds. The crowd goes wild.

I watch the next five riders perform
their routines before it's my turn. As I pedal
onto the blacktop, I'm nervous. But then
I remember what Kenzie said. *Just do your
best.* I take a deep breath. I'm ready.

The crowd cheers for me as I begin. I
do a few easy tricks at first. I do some 180
spins, a couple small wheelies, and one
move where I balance for a few seconds on
the front tire.

My moves are not as spectacular as the tricks some of the other riders did, but I'm performing them well. And I haven't fallen once.

Then I go into a more difficult trick. It's one I've been working on a lot. I stand on the front pegs, lift the back wheel off the ground, and cruise forward on just the front wheel.

I'm shaky, and I can only hold the trick for a few seconds. But still, the crowd cheers.

Finally, I'm ready for my big finish. I pedal my bike forward slowly, and then go into a front wheelie. I put the seat between my legs, lean back, and take my hands off the handle bars.

I begin to spin the bike on the front wheel. It's just like a figure skating spin. I pull my arms to my chest and feel the spin get even faster. I can hear the crowd going nuts.

I pull out of the spin and pedal to the center of the blacktop. My routine is over. I'm happy, but I don't know if I performed well enough for us to win.

I join my team for the awards ceremony.
The head judge gives the scores for flatland.
"Placing third," announces the judge, "is
Josh Champs from Victory School."

I walk up to receive my medal. I'm
happy that I placed, but I wish I had won.

I return to my team. Everyone is excited.
Kenzie gives me a big hug.

"Why are you so happy?" I ask. "I didn't
win."

"You didn't have to win," she says.

"All you needed to do was finish third," says Kirk. "That's good enough to give our team the cup!"

"You did it, Josh!" says Kenzie. "You did it!"

I watch as the final scores are posted. Sure enough, just like my teammates said, my score gives us the championship.

I helped my BMX team win the Metro Games cup. I didn't fly through the air once, but I helped us soar to victory!

GLOSSARY

180 (WHUN-ay-tee)—a trick that involves spinning 180 degrees — or a half rotation — in midair

360 (THREE-siks-tee)—a trick that involves spinning 360 degrees — or a full rotation — in midair

awesome (AW-suhm)—causing a feeling of respect and amazement

ceremony (SER-uh-moh-nee)—a formal event to mark something important

confident (KON-fuh-duhnt)—having a strong belief in one's abilities

halfpipe (HAF-pipe)—a U-shaped ramp, usually with a flat section in the middle

spectacular (spek-TAK-yuh-lur)—remarkable or dramatic

vert event (VURT i-VENT)—a competition in BMX riding and other extreme sports that involves riding on a larger version of a halfpipe

CHRIS KREIE

Chris Kreie lives in Minnesota with his wife and two children. He works as a school librarian and writes books in his free time. Some of his other books include *There Are No Figure Eights in Hockey* and *Who Wants to Play Just for Kicks?* from the Victory School Superstars series and *The Curse of Raven Lake* and *Wild Hike*.

JORGE SANTILLAN

Jorge Santillan got his start illustrating in the children's sections of local newspapers. He opened his own illustration studio in 2005. His creative team specializes in books, comics, and children's magazines. Jorge lives in Mendoza, Argentina, with his wife, Bety; son, Luca; and their four dogs, Fito, Caro, Angie, and Sammy.

FREESTYLE BMX IN HISTORY

LATE 1800S
Acrobats begin doing tricks on bicycles.

1963
Schwinn begins selling the Sting-Ray bike model. It is easy to handle, and doing wheelies becomes popular.

1975
Photos of BMX riders riding in empty swimming pools are published in *Skateboarder Magazine*.

1978
Bob Haro and R.L. Osborn form the first freestyle BMX team, which performs tricks at demonstrations.

1982
The Amateur Skate Park Association is formed. The group promotes freestyle BMX competitions.

1984
Freestylin' magazine is published for the first time. Freestyle BMX gains popularity.

1986
Fourteen-year-old Mat Hoffman joins the Haro demo team. He becomes a professional rider three years later.

1995
BMX stunt riding is an event at the first X Games, known as Extreme Games, in Rhode Island.

2010
BMX events, like the Big Air competition, continue to be among the most popular at the X Games.

Josh Champs
Lives Up to His Name!

If you liked reading Josh's BMX adventure, check out his other sports stories.

Don't Wobble on the Wakeboard!

When it comes to wakeboarding, Josh is a quick learner. But he's not as good as his competition. Heading into his big run, he is thinking just one thing: Don't wobble on the wakeboard!

There Are No Figure Eights in Hockey

Josh is already a figure skating champion, so he is looking for a new challenge. Hockey seems perfect for his super skating. But out on the ice, Josh realizes this new sport won't be easy. After all, there are no figure eights in hockey.

Who Wants to Play Just for Kicks?

Over spring break, Josh's friends want to take time off from their sports and play soccer just for fun. Josh would rather practice hockey, but he gives the game a try. When he doesn't catch on, he wonders, "Who wants to play just for kicks?"

STONE ARCH BOOKS
a capstone imprint